Mystery Man

Keith Foley had walked into the dining room. He was wearing a dark-green sweatshirt, brown pants, and a camouflage cap. He was carrying a funny little hammer that was pointed on one end and flat on the other. He did look like one of the Seven Dwarfs.

As soon as he spotted us watching him, he froze in his tracks. Stephanie smiled brightly and waved. With a scowl on his face, Keith turned around and ran out of the room.

"Wasn't that Keith?" Kate asked as she sat down at the table again.

Stephanie nodded. Then she looked at me and giggled.

"Come on, Stephanie. Eat your breakfast and give Keith Foley a rest," Kate said sternly.

"I wish I could figure out what's going on with him," Patti said, sliding into her chair. "He's a real mystery man. . . ."

Look for these and other books
in the Sleepover Friends Series:

Kate's Crush

Susan Saunders

AN
APPLE
PAPERBACK

SCHOLASTIC INC.
New York Toronto London Auckland Sydney

ISBN 0-590-42366-5

Copyright © 1989 by Daniel Weiss Associates, Inc. All rights reserved. Published by Scholastic Inc. APPLE PAPERBACKS is a registered trademark of Scholastic Inc. SLEEPOVER FRIENDS is a trademark of Scholastic Inc.

12 11 10 9 8 7 6 5 4 3 2 1   9/8 0 1 2 3 4/9

Printed in the U.S.A.   28

First Scholastic printing, September 1989

Chapter
1

"Nana loves it — she goes every year," Steph-anie Green was saying. "It's the Lost Valley Dude Ranch in Arizona. Nana wants to take all four of us with her during end-of-term break." Nana is what Stephanie calls her grandmother, Mrs. Bricker.

Stephanie, Kate Beekman, Patti Jenkins, and I sat on the floor in Kate's bedroom, finishing off some Chinese take-out from Ben Luck's. Stephanie had brought a booklet about Lost Valley Ranch from home. Patti was flipping through its pages. "It sounds neat!" she exclaimed. "Rafting down the Pearl River, nature hikes, trail rides. . . I just love horses! I used to ride in the park in the city with my mom and dad."

"Me, too," Stephanie said. "What about you

1

guys? Have you ever done any riding?" she asked Kate Beekman and me — I'm Lauren Hunter.

"No, but I've always wanted to," I said. I shut my eyes and imagined myself galloping across the desert on a black stallion. . . .

There was just one tiny problem. Lost Valley Dude Ranch is about two thousand miles from Riverhurst. Nana always took an airplane to get there. I'm not wild about airplanes. "Isn't it going to be awfully expensive?" I asked, hedging.

"Nana's paying for the cabin, of course," Stephanie said, taking a bite of sweet-and-sour shrimp. "But we will have to pay for the air fare."

Air fare — there it was again. I'm not usually the nervous type. I've jumped off the high board at the pool lots of times. I've even gone rock-climbing with my dad and my brother, Roger, so it's not heights that bother me. I guess I just think that if people were meant to fly, they'd be born with wings.

"I don't know if my parents will let me — they're trying to save . . . ," I began.

Stephanie interrupted me. "Ask them to give you the ticket for your birthday!" she said, knowing my eleventh was coming up.

Kate looked at me. "It's the flying, isn't it, Lau-

2

ren?" She pointed a barbecued spare rib at me. "How many times have you flown?"

I counted. "Uh . . . six. I've flown to Maine and back twice with my Grandmother Hunter to see Aunt Beth and Uncle Jim. That makes four flights. And I flew once with my parents and Roger to Boston and back."

"And nothing bad happened, right?" Kate said.

"No," I admitted reluctantly.

"The wheels on the plane folded up and came down just like they were supposed to, "Kate went on, one blonde eyebrow raised. "The wings didn't fall off, nothing caught on fire. . . ."

"No. I just had the feeling we were going to drop like a stone the whole time, that's all," I replied glumly.

"You're letting your imagination run away with you again," Kate said. "Be logical — everybody knows it's a thousand times safer to travel in a plane than in a car."

Sometimes Kate is so logical, it's maddening!

Stephanie giggled. "Besides, if we *drove* to Lost Valley, it would take us about four days to get there and four days to get back, which would leave us about four minutes to spend at the ranch itself."

3

"Since when have you been so interested in spending time in the great outdoors?" I asked Stephanie, who's a city kid if ever there was one.

"Take a look out the window, and tell me what you see," said Stephanie.

Millions of snowflakes were swirling around the Beekmans' house that Friday night. The wind was blowing so hard it rattled the windowpanes. I knew snow was piling up in drifts on all the sidewalks, just waiting for someone to go out and shovel it in the sub-zero weather. "A blizzard," I said.

"The second blizzard this month," Stephanie pointed out. "It's about sixty degrees warmer in Lost Valley than it is here — need I say more?"

"Not to mention it'll drive Jenny Carlin crazy," Kate added shrewdly.

Jenny Carlin's a girl in 5B, our class at Riverhurst Elementary School. She doesn't much like any of us — especially me. Ever since Jenny and I had this run-in over Pete Stone, a boy in our class, she hasn't been able to stand me. I'm afraid the feeling is definitely mutual.

Patti said, "I heard her bragging again about what fun she'll have visiting her grandmother in Florida."

"Come on, Lauren," Stephanie urged. "Horse-back riding, sunshine, driving Jenny crazy. . . ."

"I don't know. . . ," I said slowly, looking out at the snowflakes whipping past Kate's window.

"Mind over matter, Lauren," Kate said firmly.

"Easy for you to say," I mumbled. Kate really believes you can do anything if you put your mind to it.

"Lauren, you've got to come," Stephanie said. "One for all and all for one, right?"

"Right — we won't go without you, Lauren," Patti added.

"Okay, okay," I agreed at last. "I'll talk to my parents. Maybe if I borrow Roger's rabbit's foot, and take my lucky coin, the one we found at Dr. Porter's cabin, and — "

"Lau-ren!" Kate groaned, shaking her head.

Kate doesn't believe in lucky coins any more than she believes in vampires or werewolves. Wouldn't you think some of her good sense would have rubbed off on me after all these years?

Kate and I both live on Pine Street. We're practically next-door neighbors, and we started playing together when we were still babies. By kindergarten, we were best friends. That's when the sleepovers started.

Every Friday night, either I'd sleep over at Kate's house, or she'd sleep over at mine. Soon Kate's dad nicknamed us the Sleepover Twins. In those days, we thought dressing up in our moms' clothes was fabulous entertainment. "Cooking" meant making cherry Kool-Pops in the ice-cube trays, using Dr. Beekman's tongue depressors for sticks.

When we got older our cooking got better, thank goodness. Kate perfected her super-fudge, and I invented my great onion-soup-olives-bacon-bits-and-sour-cream dip. When we weren't cooking, we were spying on my older brother, Roger, and his friends, or trying to keep Kate's little sister, Melissa, from spying on *us*. We played thousands of games of Mad Libs. And because Kate's a real movie freak, we also watched every movie we could find on TV — especially every single sci-fi or horror flick that came on. I'd watch them with my hands over my eyes, because once I've *seen* them, I have nightmares about them for months!

But not Kate. She doesn't have a runaway imagination, the way I do. Nothing scares her. "Logical" should be her middle name. In fact, the two of us are totally different. She's super-neat, and I'm hopelessly messy. She doesn't like sports, and I'm kind of a jock. She's organized, and no one has ever accused me of that! We don't look anything alike, either. Kate's short and blonde, I'm tall with dark hair.

For all of our differences, though, I can't remember ever having had a serious argument with Kate . . . until Stephanie Green moved to Riverhurst from the city, the summer before fourth grade.

I got to know Stephanie because she and I were both in 4A — Mr. Civello's class — last year. Stephanie was fun. She knew all the latest dance steps. She already had her own style of dressing, too — like always wearing red, black, and white, which looks great with her dark, curly hair. And I loved hearing about the things she'd done when she lived in the city. I wanted Kate to get to know Stephanie, too, so I asked her to a sleepover at my house.

Talk about bad ideas! Kate thought Stephanie was an air-head who was only interested in shopping. Stephanie thought Kate was a stuffy know-it-all. My brother, Roger, said the problem was obvious: "They're too much alike — both bossy!"

But I was absolutely determined that all three of

us would be friends. Since we all live on Pine Street, we naturally started riding our bikes to school together. Then Stephanie asked Kate and me to a sleepover at her house, and finally, Kate invited Stephanie to one at hers. Little by little, the Sleepover Twins became a threesome.

Not that Kate and Stephanie suddenly agreed about everything, not by a long shot! They still found plenty to argue about, and I was usually caught in the middle. Then Patti Jenkins turned up in Mrs. Mead's fifth-grade class this year, along with the rest of us.

Although Patti's from the city, too, she couldn't be less like Stephanie. Patti's as quiet and shy as Stephanie is bubbly and outgoing. But Stephanie had known Patti back in the city, and she wanted her to be part of our gang. "It would kind of even things out," she had said. Kate and I both liked Patti right away. She's smart, kind, and thoughtful. And before long there were *four* Sleepover Friends!

"I can't eat another bite," Kate was saying. She began piling all the little white Chinese-food cartons on a tray.

"What about the fortune cookies?" Patti asked,

picking up the little brown bag they came in.

"Why not?" Stephanie reached for one, and so did the rest of us.

Kate broke hers open and read the slip of paper inside. " 'A refreshing change is in your future.' "

"Going to Lost Valley Dude Ranch?" Stephanie suggested.

"These things are so dumb," Kate said. "There's bound to be a change some time in my future. After all, I'm only *eleven*!"

"Mine says, 'The color green will be important to you.' " Patti giggled. "I look *awful* in green. What does yours say, Stephanie?"

" 'Friends will turn to you in affairs of the heart . . . ,' " Stephanie read slowly. "Hey — that's true! Just last week, Sally Mason" — she's another girl in our class — "asked me to tell Charlie Garner" — a boy in 5C — "that she liked him, and he said . . ."

Kate groaned. She's always after Stephanie for thinking about boys so much. "What does your cookie say, Lauren?" Kate asked.

" 'You can solve your problem if you exert yourself,' " I read. "I think *you* wrote this one, Kate!"

"That's the first fortune cookie I've run across

9

that makes any sense," Kate said, nodding in approval.

"How about it, Lauren?" Stephanie said.

"Are we going to Lost Valley?" Patti added.

Maybe I could think of it as a game of Truth or Dare. The plane flight would be the dare of my life! "Why not?" I said as coolly as I could. "I can handle it."

Chapter 2

I didn't feel nearly so cool three weeks later. Nana, Stephanie, Kate, Patti, and I were sitting with our luggage in a tiny plane — barely big enough for the five of us — on a narrow runway outside of a little town named Antelope Creek.

"Buckle up, girls, it's the last leg of our trip," Nana said cheerfully as we waited for the engine to warm up.

The propellers began spinning faster and faster and the plane started to bump down the runway. "I'm beginning to think that Lost Valley is going to *stay* lost!" Stephanie grumbled to me. "First, we crammed into cars in Riverhurst and drove to the airport in the city. Then we got on a crowded jet and flew thousands of miles. Then we piled into a dusty van, and now we're on this thing. . . . My clothes are totally wrinkled, my hair is frizzing. I'm a total wreck. . . . When will it ever end?''

I didn't answer. I was too busy clutching the arms of my seat and trying not to think about the fact that I was stuck in a tiny plane in the middle of nowhere with no hope of escape.

"We're in the air!" Kate announced after one last horrible jolt. She and Patti were sitting across the narrow aisle from Stephanie and me.

Patti pressed her face to the window. "The clouds look like huge snowbanks," she said.

"Then why aren't they s-smoother?" I complained, squeezing my eyes shut. The plane was bouncing around like a Ping-Pong ball.

"We're experiencing just a little turbulence, folks," came the pilot's voice from the cockpit.

"No kidding," I muttered.

"We'll be out of it in a second," the pilot added soothingly.

"I think you'd feel better if you opened your eyes, Lauren dear," Nana said from the seat behind me.

"We're not even that high, Lauren," Kate reported. "We're flying over sand and rocks and cactus — and I think I see a herd of deer!" she added excitedly.

"Pronghorn antelopes," Nana told us. "And there's the beginning of Lost Valley!"

I opened my eyes. Nana was right — I did feel a little less dizzy.

"I can't believe it!" Stephanie said, peering through the square window next to my seat. "Wow — it's already night down there!"

"That's the Lost Valley," Nana said with a smile.

I finally took a look myself. The reddish-brown sand of the desert stretched out as flat as a plate, with a scattering of rocks and straggly tan bushes here and there. It looked as if an enormous green crack had split the desert open right under our plane.

Where we were, the sun was still shining, although it hung low in the sky. But the canyon below us was filled with shadows and dark green trees. The twisty silver river running through it glittered like glass.

"The Pearl River," Nana said. "It flows down from the mountains to the north."

"It's beautiful," I said, loosening my grip on the arms of my seat.

As we flew over it, the canyon widened until it was large enough to hold a handful of houses with lights twinkling in the windows.

"There's the ranch," Nana announced. "The airstrip is just past it. Now we'll swing around and start to come down. . . ."

"Ulp!" My stomach threatened to take a nose-dive, and I grabbed my seat again as the little plane swung into a U-turn. We dropped down . . . down . . . past pink sandstone cliffs and tall, narrow trees. Then we glided over the silvery river and aimed for the airstrip, lit by bright blue lights. We touched the runway, wobbled for a minute or two, then braked slowly to a stop.

The pilot turned off the engine and opened the door of the plane.

"We actually made it!" I murmured. I took a deep breath.

The air was dry and warm, and it smelled like pine trees and woodsmoke and lots of other good things.

"Our safe trip was undoubtedly the work of the rabbit's foot and your lucky coin," Kate said with a wry smile.

Then a voice boomed out, "Welcome to Lost

Valley Ranch!" A big man in a gray ten-gallon hat was grinning through the door at us.

"Howdy, Mrs. Bricker — welcome back!" the tall cowboy said. "If you'll all just climb down, I'll get your bags into that wagon." He pointed to the side of the airstrip. There really *was* a wagon parked there pulled by two caramel-colored horses. "Then we'll mosey over to your cabin before we go to the Lodge," he went on. He guided Mrs. Bricker down the steps of the plane and introduced himself to the rest of us. "I'm Buck Walters, and I help out Mrs. Franklin. She's the owner of Lost Valley Ranch. I'm the foreman on the ranch and the trail boss."

"This is my granddaughter, Stephanie," Mrs. Bricker told Buck. "And these are her best friends, Patti, Lauren, and Kate."

Buck touched his hat brim and shook hands with each of us. His hands were huge and rough from working outside.

"Are you the one who takes people on trail rides?" Stephanie asked him.

"That's right, just as soon as you get used to our saddle horses, and they get used to you," Buck replied. He had a grayish-blond mustache that curled up at the ends when he smiled.

15

He tossed our heavy suitcases in the back of the wagon as easily as if they were completely empty, instead of crammed with practically everything we owned. Then he helped Nana onto the seat and climbed up next to her.

Stephanie, Kate, Patti, and I peeled off our heavy jackets and scarves and sat down in the back of the wagon, our legs dangling over the dirt road.

Buck lifted the reins, made a clicking sound to the horses, and off we went.

Chapter
3

"I feel as though we're in a western movie!" Patti said as the wagon rolled along the winding dirt road, the horses' harnesses jingling. "The kind of western where the family's going to town to do their shopping for the first time in six months!"

"How depressing!" Stephanie put in, staring down the dark, empty road. She practically lives at the mall back in Riverhurst. "It does look kind of deserted. . . ."

"Well, it is very *warm* here," Kate reminded her.

It was true. It was the dead of winter, a soft breeze was blowing.

"How old are you girls? About twelve?" Buck asked over his shoulder.

Needless to say, it's a lot nicer to be guessed *older* than you are than *younger* than you are.

"Just about," Stephanie answered, although she'd barely had her eleventh birthday.

"That's what I figured," Buck said. "There's a young feller about your age staying at the lodge with his grandparents, the Foleys. I'll bet he's going to be glad to have some company."

"A real boy, all the way out here!" Stephanie exclaimed to Kate, Patti, and me. "I hope he's cute!"

Kate rolled her eyes, the way she always does when Stephanie starts talking about boys. But she didn't have time to say anything, because just then the wagon pulled up in front of a little cabin set in a grove of evergreens.

"Here we are, ladies," Buck said.

"It's darling!" Stephanie said.

The porch light was on, so we could see that the cabin itself was made of thick, gray logs. It was one-story tall, and had little square windows, a high peaked roof, and smoke curling out of the chimney. On the screened-in porch next to the front door was a stack of firewood.

Buck jumped down from the wagon. He grabbed a couple of suitcases and clomped up the steps. He pushed open the screen door and then the front door, which he held for Nana. Then Stephanie, Kate, Patti, and I followed him inside.

The living room took up most of the cabin. Woven Indian rugs in bright colors covered the floor. Two couches and some comfortable chairs were arranged around a fireplace, where a fire was already blazing away. Nana said that we actually needed a fire because at night the temperature in the valley dropped way down.

Behind a door at one end of the big living room was a bathroom, with an old-fashioned bathtub with claw feet. Through a second door was a small bedroom, with two sets of bunk beds, and a chair and table made of thin logs with the bark still on them.

The bedroom windows opened out onto one side of the canyon. You could hear the river flowing not far away. And if you looked up, you could see all the colors of the sunset — orange, red, purple — showing above the top of a pink cliff.

"There are only four beds," Kate pointed out. "Who's sleeping where?"

"If you girls can manage on the bunks," Nana called from the big room, "I'll be very comfortable here on one of these pull-out couches."

"I don't want to hurry you ladies," Buck said as he set down the last of the suitcases. "But it's almost suppertime."

Suppertime! My stomach had definitely bounced back from the plane ride, because suddenly, I was *starving*. Everybody else was hungry, too. We quickly pulled on light sweaters, and piled back into the wagon.

Buck pointed out the sights as we jingled up the road toward the lodge. "The low building on the right is the stable," he told us. "The tack room's at the end of it — that's where you'll get your saddles and bridles and other equipment."

"I think I can hear the horses," Patti said.

"Yep — they're begging for their supper," Buck said with a grin. "Just past the stable, behind those trees, there are four more little cabins like yours. On the other side of the road is the bunkhouse, where the ranch hands live." The long log cabin had a stone chimney at each end. "And next to it," said Buck pointing, "is my house, and here's the lodge, in front of us."

Buck guided the horses up a narrow, curved driveway. "Whoa," he said, and the wagon came to a stop next to a huge two-story house.

"More logs," Stephanie said.

"That's about all there was to build with in the old days — cedar trees," Buck replied. "Now just go right on up those steps. I expect I'll see you girls bright and early tomorrow morning at the stables."

"You bet," Stephanie said enthusiastically. I had my doubts — Stephanie's not exactly an early riser.

"Good night, Buck," said Nana. "Thank you."

The five of us climbed a long flight of wooden stairs to a wide front porch lined with rocking chairs. Mrs. Franklin was waiting for us.

Mrs. Franklin was a short, round woman with curly gray hair, a tanned face, and a warm smile. "We heard your plane landing," she said. "I'm so glad to see you back with us, Mrs. Bricker." She gave Nana a peck on the cheek.

"This must be your granddaughter," Mrs. Franklin went on, giving Stephanie a hug. "I remember your grandmother talking about your favorite colors when she was here last time." Stephanie had on black jeans and a red, black, and white sweatshirt, so it wasn't too hard to pick her out.

After she'd met everyone, Mrs. Franklin led us into the Lodge's large living room. The ceiling stretched from a second-floor balcony up to the peaked roof. One two-story wall had been made into a floor-to-ceiling bookcase. The other one was covered with animal heads — deer, some of the little antelopes Kate had seen from the plane, buffalos, and even a bear!

"Eeeuuu!" Stephanie exclaimed.

"How awful!" Patti murmured.

"Those are left over from the days when this was really a hunting lodge," Mrs. Franklin explained. "That was way before my time. Now the only hunting we do is with cameras."

I think all of us felt better after we heard that.

"Come on," Mrs. Franklin said. "I don't want your supper to get cold."

Almost every inch of space in the dining room was taken up by big, square wooden tables and the leather chairs around them. The other guests at Lost Valley Ranch were already sitting down, having their soup.

Mrs. Franklin pointed out a young blond couple on the other side of the room. "Those are the Putnams," she told us. "They're on their honeymoon." The Putnams smiled and waved. The Murrays, sitting at the same table, were an older couple. They were wearing matching western shirts.

Mr. Kessler, a nice-looking man about Nana's age, sat at a table with a couple named the Denmans. Then there were two more tables of four people each, but I couldn't keep all their names straight — until we got to the Foleys, that is.

Mrs. Foley was a cheerful-looking lady with short, reddish-blonde hair. Mr. Foley had a gray crewcut, and he wore wire-rimmed glasses. The boy sitting with them was looking out the window with his back to us.

"And this is their grandson, Keith," Mrs. Franklin went on. "Keith's interested in fossils. That's why he's come to Lost Valley — we've got plenty of them. I bet he'd like to tell you all about it after dinner."

Keith Foley had short, wavy brown hair, he was kind of stocky — I knew *I* would tower over him, and Patti's even taller than I am. But that was all I could see, because Keith Foley didn't turn around, even when Mrs. Franklin tried to introduce us.

"Keith!" Mrs. Foley scolded. She reached out and jiggled his arm.

Keith turned his head then, just a fraction.

"He looks a little like Kyle Hubbard," Kate said under her breath. Kyle's a guy back in Riverhurst.

He and Kate got to be friends when they were in the same fourth-grade class last year.

"Hi!" all four of us said at once. Keith had a squarish face and big brown eyes. He was kind of cute, but he wasn't exactly what you'd call friendly. He barely bothered to nod before giving us the cold shoulder again.

"Well!" Stephanie muttered.

Maybe Keith did look a little like Kyle Hubbard. But he certainly *didn't* look like a boy who wanted to tell us all about fossils after dinner. He looked more like a boy who wanted us all to drop through the floor!

Chapter
4

Mrs. Franklin and Nana exchanged glances. Then Mrs. Franklin said quickly, "Here's an empty table for the four girls, right next to the Foleys, and Mrs. Bricker, why don't you sit over here with the Denmans and Mr. Kessler?"

"No way I'm sitting close to *him*," I murmured as Mrs. Franklin pulled out our chairs. Keith glared at us out of the corner of his eye.

"Me, neither," Stephanie said in a low voice. "If looks could kill, we'd be hanging up on that wall next to the bear and the buffalo. . . ."

"Then I guess I'll sit next to him," Kate said. She sounded totally disgusted with us.

She plopped down on the chair closest to Keith

Foley. Then I sat on her left. Patti sat on her right, and Stephanie sat across from her. On the other side of the dining room, Mr. Kessler held out an empty chair for Nana.

While Mrs. Franklin served us our cheese soup, Mr. and Mrs. Foley leaned over and spoke to Kate. But Keith acted as if she weren't there. He just hunched over the table with his soup in front of him, digging around in it with his spoon as if he expected to uncover a dinosaur bone or something.

Supper was great — a big smoked ham with pineapple slices all over it, baked potatoes with sour cream, homemade biscuits, and cherry pie for dessert. But Keith didn't open his mouth the whole time. He just scowled and played with the food on his plate.

By the time supper was over, it had gotten much cooler. Some of the other guests gathered around the fireplace that had been built in the living room and began to talk. Nana and the four of us decided to walk back to our cabin and go to bed.

"I think we're all pretty tired after our trip," Nana told Mr. Kessler and the Foleys.

"And we want to get up early and go riding tomorrow," Patti added.

"Plus we won't have to hang around being glared at by Keith Foley!" whispered Stephanie, watching him out of the corner of her eye. He turned away and stared out the window again.

"Riding! Hear that, Keith?" said Mrs. Foley. "Why don't you try it, too?"

Keith sighed impatiently. Then, without a word, he stamped toward the stairs to the second-floor rooms.

Mr. Foley shrugged apologetically, and we all said good night.

"Maybe he doesn't talk because he has an odd voice," Patti said softly as we walked down the steps outside.

"Yeah — high and stuttery," Stephanie said. "You know — like Porky Pig or something!"

All of us started giggling.

"Perhaps he's just shy, Stephanie," Nana said to her granddaughter.

"It's more than that," I said. "He didn't eat a thing all through dinner. Not even a bite of the ham. There must be something wrong with him!"

"Maybe he just wasn't hungry," Kate said.

"Not hungry?" I exclaimed.

"It does happen, Lauren," Kate said dryly.

27

"I'll bet he's chicken," Stephanie cut in.

"What do you mean?" Kate asked.

"Afraid of horses, for one thing. Did you see the way he ran off when his grandparents tried to get him to go riding? He's probably afraid of girls, too," Stephanie added with a sniff. If there's one thing she hates, it's being ignored. "He may be as cute as Kyle Hubbard, but I think he's a wimp."

"Stephanie, you have no way of knowing that," Nana said, turning on the flashlight Mrs. Franklin had lent her.

"Right — maybe he's just the strong, silent type," Kate teased.

"No way," Stephanie said positively, and she walked on ahead. "He's afraid to talk to me."

The moon was rising over the canyon wall, and the night sky was sprinkled with the brightest stars I'd ever seen. A long, spooky howl echoed in the distance, joined by another, and another.

"Wh-what was that?" Stephanie said. She and Patti and I moved closer together.

"Don't you remember your western movies?" Kate said excitedly. "I'll bet it's coyotes!"

"That's right," Nana said. "They're serenading the moon."

"Not the pack of werewolves you guys were imagining," Kate giggled. "Maybe Keith's not the only chicken."

The coyotes howled again. Even though I knew what the noises were this time, a shiver ran down my spine. "I guess new things can be kind of scary," I said, sympathizing with Keith a little.

"New things like girls and horses?" Stephanie said. "Give me a break." But I noticed she edged even closer to Patti and me all the way back to the cabin.

The four of us had planned to stay awake and talk that night, but as soon as I put my head on my pillow, I went out like a light. I didn't wake up until there was a knock at our window early the next morning.

Kate just groaned, covering her head with her blanket.

"M-mph?" Patti said, and turned over — she was on a top bunk, above Kate.

Stephanie mumbled something in her sleep and burrowed deeper under the covers.

I managed to open my eyes and push the curtains aside. I peered out into the pale gray morning light and saw Buck Walters standing outside our cabin.

"I thought you girls might like to watch us break a colt," he said, after I'd managed to push the window open a crack.

"Break a colt?" I asked, rubbing my eyes.

"That means getting him used to being ridden," Buck explained.

"*I* would!" I said.

"Me, too," Patti agreed, forcing herself to sit up.

Kate and Stephanie mumbled that they'd come, too.

"Fine — why don't you run up to the lodge and grab yourselves some breakfast," Buck said. "I'll meet you at the pens. They're right behind the stable." Then he strolled away, his brown chaps — these leather trousers cowboys wear over their jeans for protection — flapping around his long legs.

Patti and I got dressed in about two minutes flat. It took Kate and Stephanie a little longer. But finally all four of us crept through the big room where Nana was sleeping and out the door.

As we headed up the road, Stephanie looked down at her watch. "Six-thirty!" she groaned. "That's practically the middle of the night!"

"It's eight-thirty in Riverhurst," I pointed out.

"Besides, we don't want to miss anything."

Stephanie made a face.

"You were the one who wanted to get up bright and early," Kate pointed out.

"At least we know the stable is one place we won't have to put up with Keith Foley's bad manners," Stephanie said, to cheer herself up.

Everybody perked up when we got to the dining room at the lodge. No one was around except us, but there was plenty of food waiting on the warming trays, including Mrs. Franklin's delicious homemade muffins.

Kate and Patti had gone back for seconds when Stephanie suddenly jabbed me with her elbow. "I was wrong about Keith being like Porky Pig," she hissed. "He's really one of the Seven Dwarfs." Softly, she started whistling the song the dwarfs sing in *Snow White* on their way to work in the mines.

"What are you talking about?" I said.

Stephanie nodded toward the door.

Keith Foley had walked into the dining room. He was wearing a dark-green sweatshirt, brown pants, and a camouflage cap. He was carrying a funny little hammer that was pointed on one end and flat on the other. His outfit did remind me a little of the dwarfs in the movie. On the other hand, he really was kind of cute.

As soon as he spotted us watching him he froze in his tracks. Stephanie smiled brightly and waved. With a scowl on his face, Keith turned around and dashed out of the room.

"Wasn't that Keith?" Kate asked as she sat down at the table again.

Stephanie nodded and quietly sang, "Heigh ho, it's off to work we go." Then she looked at me and giggled.

"Come on, Stephanie. Eat your breakfast, and give Keith Foley a rest," Kate said sternly.

"I wish I could figure out what's going on with him," Patti said, sliding into her chair. "He's a real mystery man, which makes him kind of interesting. . . ."

I knew what she meant. In spite of myself, I wanted to know what Keith's story was, too. Why wouldn't he talk? Or eat? Did he just hate girls or what?

As soon as we finished our breakfast, the four of us hurried outside and down to the stables. Buck Walters was leaning against a fence.

"Good morning," he said as we walked up. "You're just in time for the show. That's Wacy, in the blue shirt, and the colt he's on is called Smokey."

We peered over the fence. Two cowboys were holding the bridle of a big gray horse. A young red-headed cowboy in a blue shirt was sitting in the saddle, gripping the reins tightly. Then he nodded and said, "Okay — turn 'im loose!"

The cowboys on the ground took their hands off the bridle and stepped back. Smokey stood stock-still for a second. Then he shot into the air like a rocket. He hit the ground so hard I thought Wacy was going to go flying. But he managed to hold on.

"Keep his head up!" Buck shouted to Wacy, who was pulling on the reins with all his might.

"Wow!" Stephanie cried. "A one-horse roller coaster!"

"How does he stay on?" Patti wondered out loud.

But Wacy did stay on, no matter what Smokey tried — until the colt decided to race full speed around the pen, and then stop dead in his tracks! Wacy hurtled over the saddle horn, and hit the ground with a solid *thud*!

He just lay there for a second, not even twitching, while Smokey made a rude noise with his nose and looked pleased with himself.

"Is Wacy. . . ," Kate began worriedly.

But the other two cowboys were laughing as they helped Wacy to his feet. "He sure planted you, Wace," one of them said.

"Knocked the wind plumb out of me," Wacy gasped with a grin.

"So — you girls ready to try it?" Buck asked us.

"Not on him," Stephanie said, pointing to Smokey.

"Nope, I think we'll start you out on something a little calmer," Buck said, smiling broadly. "Come on into the stable."

He opened the door to the first stall. "Stephanie, I'm giving you Maxine, because you and she kind of go together," he said, glancing at Stephanie's black-and-white striped sweatshirt. Maxine was a black horse with white legs and a white stripe running down her face.

Buck handed Stephanie the halter rope. "Lead her down the alley to the tack room, and we'll saddle up," he told her.

My horse was reddish-brown, with big brown

eyes and black lashes. He ambled out of his stall and practically yawned in my face. Not exactly the black stallion I'd imagined myself riding, but I guess you have to start somewhere. "Was this horse ever as lively as Smokey?" I asked.

"Well, some colts are a little friskier than others," Buck replied. "This is Greedy. . . ."

"Grady?" I repeated.

"No — *Greedy*, because he eats us out of house and home," Buck said.

I was waiting for Kate to say that he was the perfect horse for me. I have what *I* call a healthy appetite, and everybody else calls the bottomless pit.

But Kate didn't say anything. It wasn't like her to pass up a chance like that. In fact, she'd been awfully quiet for the past few minutes. I looked over at her. She was standing near the stable door, and she looked kind of pale. "Are you okay?" I asked.

"Sure," she said, turning to peer into a stall. "Which is my horse, Buck?"

Buck gave Kate a big friendly palomino named Sal. Patti would be riding a tall brown horse called Timber.

First, Buck showed us how to curry our horses with a flat rubber brush so that their coats gleamed.

Then he taught us how to saddle and bridle them.

"You can tell a lot from a horse's ears," Buck said as he helped Kate slip her bridle over Sal's head. "When they're both pointing forward, she's interested in what's going on in front of her. But if they're both lying back, look out, she's about to start something."

"Start something?" Kate said, staring at her horse's ears.

Buck nodded. "Biting, or kicking, maybe — definitely something no good."

"What do you do?" Stephanie asked.

"Yell at the horse, or jerk the reins to get his attention. You have to show him who's boss," Buck advised.

"What about when one ear is forward, and the other one is back?" I asked, which is how Greedy's ears were then.

"He's listening to you, in a sleepy sort of way," Buck said with a grin. "Ready? Let's lead them outside."

Once we were out of the stable, our riding lesson started for real.

"You always mount a horse from his left side. Grab the saddlehorn with your left hand and put your left foot in the stirrup," Buck told Kate and me, since Patti and Stephanie already knew how. "Okay — now grab the cantle of your saddle — that's the back part of it — with your right hand, and pull yourself up."

I watched Patti and Stephanie swinging their right legs over their horses' backs, and I did the same thing. I was actually sitting on top of a large, warm, furry horse. It was incredible!

Buck readjusted our stirrups so they'd be the correct length: He shortened Kate's and Stephanie's and made Patti's and mine longer. "Everybody comfortable?" he said. "In western riding, you sit way back in the saddle. Then you relax, and try to move with your horse. Now give 'im a little nudge with your legs . . . that's right."

Stephanie and Patti's horses walked forward. Greedy stayed right where he was. "Greedy probably needs a little more than a nudge," he said. Buck looked at me and chuckled. "In fact, a good kick wouldn't hurt."

I gave Greedy's fat sides a gentle kick with my heels . . . it worked. I was *riding a horse*, swaying from side to side as Greedy put one foot forward, and then another.

"Reins in your right hand, left hand on the horn if you feel safer that way," Buck called. "Steer him toward the pen."

I was so excited that I didn't think about Kate, until I heard her voice behind me. "Maybe I'd better get down," she said.

"Just pull on the reins," Buck told her.

I pulled on mine, too — Greedy was a lot easier to stop than to get started. I twisted around in my saddle in time to see Buck helping Kate dismount. "Is something wrong?" he asked her.

Kate's face looked as pale as Pearl River. "Uh — I'm getting a headache," she said, frowning a little in the bright sunlight. "It's probably an allergy," she added.

"What's the matter?" Stephanie and Patti had turned their horses around and ridden back.

"Kate's allergic to something," I replied. But I was puzzled. Usually Kate sneezes when she's allergic to something. I couldn't remember her ever having a headache.

"I think I'll go back to the cabin," Kate murmured to Buck. "I'll lie down for a minute, until my head feels better."

"Do you want us to come with you?" I asked her.

Kate shook her head. "No, I'll be okay. You should just finish your lesson." She handed Sal's reins to Buck. Then, still frowning, she walked away from the stable.

Chapter 5

Stephanie, Patti, and I rode around inside the pen, getting used to our horses.

"Turn 'em to the left," Buck called out. "Pull the reins tight against the right side of their necks. Good! Now to the right . . . make 'em *mind* you. The horse has to go where *you* want him to go, Lauren — not where *he* wants to go," Buck added as Greedy veered off toward the gate.

When the sun really started to warm things up in the canyon, Buck decided we'd had enough.

"All three of you did great," he said. "I'll unsaddle the horses. Why don't you run on up to the lodge? I'll bet Mrs. Franklin has a big pitcher of iced tea waiting."

As soon as I slid off Greedy's broad back, I realized I wasn't going to *run* anyplace. Once my feet were on the ground, I felt as bowlegged as a bulldog. About all I could manage was a slow waddle. But I loved riding. I couldn't believe how much fun it was. "Will you give us another lesson this afternoon, Buck?" I asked.

"Nope — this afternoon Wacy's going to paddle you down the river," Buck said as he took the horses' reins.

"That sounds nice and cool," Stephanie said, pushing back her damp curls. "Let's go for that tea."

"We'd better check on Kate first," Patti reminded her. She patted Timber one last time. When we got to our cabin, though, it was empty. The bunks had been made, and Kate's wasn't even wrinkled.

"I don't think she's been here at all," I said. I was kind of worried.

"Then she must be up at the lodge," said Stephanie.

We'd barely climbed the steps of the lodge when Kate came barreling out the front door. Her cheeks turned pink when she saw us. "Finished so soon?" she asked.

"It was getting hot," Stephanie answered.

"Are you feeling better, Kate?" Patti asked.

"A little," Kate said, looking down at her feet. "I came up here to get an . . . an aspirin from Mrs. Franklin . . . I'm going back to the cabin for a while."

Patti nodded. "We'll come for you when it's time for lunch, okay?"

"Okay." Kate hurried down the wooden stairs. All three of us stared after her.

"She's acting kind of weird, don't you think?" Stephanie asked.

"It's just her headache," Patti said.

"I thought she looked embarrassed." Stephanie turned to me. "Didn't you, Lauren?"

"What does she have to be embarrassed about?" I replied. But Stephanie had a point. Kate *had* blushed.

"I don't know. Let's go inside and see if we can spot any interesting reasons." Stephanie pushed the front door of the lodge open and peered in. Then she nudged me with her elbow. "Look!" she whispered.

Keith Foley was sitting on one of the couches in the big room, flipping through a book. But before we'd taken ten steps forward, he jumped up, threw the book on the coffee table, and shot up the stairs to the second floor.

"*We* may scare him, but I don't think Kate

does," Stephanie said meaningfully.

"How do you know that?" I asked her.

"That's Kate's blue cardigan hanging over the back of the couch," Stephanie said. "She and Keith must have been sitting in here together!"

It *was* Kate's sweater, and she *had* looked embarrassed, but sneaking around isn't Kate's style.

"You know what I think?" Stephanie said excitedly. "I think Kate doesn't have a headache at all — the headache was just an excuse!"

"An excuse for what?" Patti asked.

"To follow Keith up here," Stephanie said. "I think Kate *likes* him!"

"Come on, Stephanie!" I exclaimed. "Kate?"

"She said he looks like Kyle, right?" Stephanie said.

"He does look a little like Kyle," I said.

"And Kate likes Kyle," Stephanie went on, ignoring my interruption.

"Only as a friend," Patti said.

"Still. She sat in the chair closest to him at dinner," Stephanie went on.

"Only because *we* wouldn't," Patti pointed out.

"And she stuck up for him last night *and* this morning at breakfast," Stephanie said. "I'm *sure* I'm right. You know when we were getting on our horses? I saw Keith just about then, walking toward the lodge from the river carrying that dumb hammer.''

''So?'' I said.

''So Kate must have seen him, too,'' Stephanie said. ''Because she got the headache not two minutes after that! Pretty convenient, if you ask me. . . . Have you ever known Kate to have a headache?''

''Well . . . no,'' I had to agree.

''I rest my case!'' Stephanie said. Her dad's a lawyer, which is why she uses expressions like that.

Stephanie walked over to the coffee table and picked up Keith's book. *''Beginner's Guide to Western Riding''* she read aloud, and sniffed, ''That figures.'' ''It's a lot safer to read about it than try it. I never thought Kate would be interested in a wimp.''

Stephanie put the book down again, and added thoughtfully, ''Although I guess you could say Bobby Krieger's sort of wimpy.'' Bobby Krieger is a boy in 5C whom Kate used to like.

''He's just quiet,'' Patti said in Bobby's defense. ''Maybe Keith is, too.''

''If Kate were interested in Keith Foley, don't you think she would have said something about it?'' I asked Stephanie. ''Kate is very straightforward.''

"Oh, yeah?" Stephanie replied. "How long did it take her to tell us she liked Royce Mason?" Royce is a seventh-grader. "Months! Besides, she might feel funny admitting it to me. You know how she's always making fun of me for thinking about boys."

I mulled it over for a moment. "Royce and Kyle and Keith all have brown hair and brown eyes," I said slowly. "Do you think there's a pattern here?"

"Exactly!" Stephanie crowed.

Patti and I nodded.

"We always help each other out, don't we?" Stephanie rushed on. "Kate's going to need all the help she can get with this one. Remember: 'Friends will turn to you in affairs of the heart,' " She quoted from her fortune cookie with a satisfied smile.

"Kate hasn't really *turned* to us," I said doubtfully.

"Sssh!" Patti warned. "Somebody's coming!"

We could hear footsteps moving toward us from the back of the lodge. Then Mrs. Franklin peered into the room. "Here you are!" she said. "Iced tea and banana bread in the kitchen, girls."

"We'll talk about this later," Stephanie said under her breath as the three of us followed Mrs. Franklin through the dining room.

45

Chapter 6

Stephanie, Patti, and I drank about a gallon of iced tea and snacked on Mrs. Franklin's delicious banana bread. All that horseback riding had really given us an appetite. When we were stuffed, we strolled out onto the front porch of the lodge.

We'd just sat down on three of the rockers when we saw Nana coming back from a hike with the Foleys and Mr. Kessler. "It's wonderful out there!" Mr. Kessler said, taking off his green cap and fanning his face with it. "How was the horseback riding?"

"Great!" I said. "We learned how to get on a horse. We walked. We even trotted. We'll manage the trail ride with no problem!"

"Did you get any good pictures?" Patti asked

Nana. Nana's hobby is photography.

She nodded enthusiastically. "I snapped a doe and a fawn near the river. Oh, and I got a picture of an armadillo, and a racoon, too," she replied. Then she counted heads. "Where's Kate?" she asked us.

"Back at the cabin. She has an allergy headache," Patti said with a sidelong glance at Stephanie.

"Poor thing," Nana said. "Maybe I'd better go see about her."

"She took an aspirin and she's lying down until lunch," Stephanie reported. "She'll be fine."

"Have you girls seen Keith?" Mrs. Foley wondered.

"I think he's upstairs in his room," Stephanie answered.

"That boy!" Mrs. Foley said with a sigh. "I'd hoped this trip would make him forget his troubles."

Stephanie nudged me in the ribs. Something was definitely up with Keith Foley!

"We're going to raft down the river this afternoon," Stephanie said casually. "Maybe Keith would like to come along. I know we'll be seeing some fossils. . . ."

"I'll go right up and tell him about it!" Mrs. Foley said, brightening.

"Shall we look for something cool to drink?" Mr. Kessler held open the front door for Nana, and the four grown-ups went inside.

"Stephanie, he'll wreck our river trip!" I whispered.

"I'm only doing it for Kate," she said.

"What was that about fossils, anyway?" Patti asked.

Stephanie shrugged. "Mrs. Franklin said Lost Valley has plenty of them, so there are bound to be a few near the river, don't you think?"

"Well, the river probably used to fill this entire valley," Patti said. "Over millions and millions of years, the river would have cut deeper and deeper into the rock, until it ended where it is now, right at the bottom of the canyon," she told us. "I'd say there are more likely to be fossils up there." She pointed toward the top of the cliffs.

"Details, details," Stephanie sniffed. "Anyway, you can tell Kate all that at lunch, so she can convince Keith she's a real fossil expert this afternoon on the river trip. He'll be totally impressed."

"Stephanie, Kate won't like it if we mix into this," I warned. Patti nodded in agreement.

"Then just look at it as a favor to poor Keith Foley," Stephanie replied breezily. "Didn't you hear what his grandmother said? 'It would make him forget his troubles.' "

"I wonder what troubles he has?" Patti said. She's very soft hearted.

"Besides some major personality flaws?" Stephanie muttered.

"Maybe he *should* be brought out of himself a little . . . ," Patti said.

"That's it!" Stephanie cried. "We'll put a little excitement into his humdrum life. And if it helps out Kate, too . . . all the better!"

But Keith didn't come on the river trip with us, after all.

"Keith told his grandparents he'd rather hike up the canyon with them," said Nana as we helped her gather up cameras and film for the trip.

Stephanie frowned. She didn't say anything, but I could practically *hear* the wheels turning in her head.

The Murphys were out riding with Buck. The Putnams and two other couples were rock-climbing.

Just the four of us — Kate's headache was better — would be going up the river, along with Nana and Mr. Kessler.

We gathered at the small dock where the boat was waiting. Actually, it wasn't a real boat. It was one of those inflatable rubber rafts, the enormous yellow kind with three seats and an outboard motor. Mr. Kessler helped Nana onto the raft, and he carried her camera for her.

"It's nice that Nana has somebody to hang around with," Stephanie whispered. "Especially since practically every other grown-up is part of a couple."

Wacy was running the boat.

We all strapped ourselves into life jackets and took our seats. Stephanie and Patti sat in front, Kate and I in the second row, and Nana and Mr. Kessler in the back. Wacy crouched down next to the outboard. He turned on the engine and gunned it a couple of times. Then he backed away from the river bank and steered us out into the current.

We'd barely chugged past the last cabin at the ranch when we spotted the Foleys hiking through the trees to the river.

"Aho-o-oy!" Mr. Foley called out. He and his

wife waved energetically, but Keith immediately disappeared behind a tall cedar tree.

Stephanie turned around in her seat. "Keith Foley is such a Mystery Man!" she yelled over the sound of the outboard. "I can't figure him out. . . . What's he really like, Kate?" I guess she'd decided to take the direct approach.

"How would I know?" Kate exclaimed quickly. She didn't look any of us in the eye when she said it, though.

"Haven't you talked to him?" Stephanie asked innocently. "You were both sitting in the big room at the lodge this morning, weren't you? Keith was reading that horseback riding book, and — "

"I didn't even *see* Keith Foley at the lodge, much less talk to him!" Kate interrupted sharply. But her cheeks had turned a bright pink again. Stephanie was right!

Stephanie opened her mouth to add something, but Kate glared at her so hard, she shut it again.

"Hey! Look at those two antelopes near that rock!" Patti broke in quickly. "Ooops! They're gone!" My guess was that there never were any antelopes, but she'd changed the subject very nicely.

It was hard to talk over the noise of the motor,

anyway, so we stayed pretty quiet the rest of the way downriver. As we chugged along, we saw deer with beautiful horns, two eagles, and a whole family of wild pigs drinking from the water's edge. Nana snapped plenty of photographs and talked and laughed with Mr. Kessler.

The pink cliffs moved closer to the river as we traveled farther from the ranch, until there was just the water in the middle, with two huge walls of striped rock on either side. Then the river split into two forks, one flowing to the left and the other to the right. In the center was a small, sandy island.

Wacy turned off the motor, and we drifted slowly toward the island. When we were close he leaped over the side of the raft and dragged it up on the sand.

"Here's where we stop," he said, helping us all climb out. "Mrs. Franklin packed lemonade and sandwiches for a picnic." He carried the picnic basket over to a clump of willow trees.

"What is this island called?" Stephanie asked.

"It doesn't have a name," Wacy said. "Mainly because it comes and goes."

"A movable island?" Kate exclaimed.

"Depending on how high the water is in the

canyon," Wacy explained. "Sometimes more than half of the island is under water. A couple of times, it's disappeared completely."

"What's that weird white rock sticking out of the cliff up there?" Kate pointed at the canyon wall closest to us. The rock looked like a giant bullet, or the nose cone of a rocket.

"We call that Tower Rock," Wacy replied. "It's full of fossil shells, from millions of years ago when all this country was covered by oceans."

"Fossils!" Stephanie said thoughtfully. Patti and I glanced at each other. We both could tell she was planning something. "Wacy, is there any way we can get up there?"

"From here?" Wacy shook his head and grinned. "Not unless you're the Human Fly."

"Wasn't that a terrific movie?" Kate added. "Do you watch much sci-fi?" Kate's always interested in talking about movies, even on a river in the middle of nowhere.

"You bet. There's no television down here in the canyon — the signals can't get to us — but we do have a VCR at the bunkhouse," Wacy said.

"Arrr-hmmm!" Stephanie cleared her throat loudly to steer him back to *her* subject. "I didn't mean

53

get there from *here*," she said firmly. "I meant could we ride to Tower Rock from the ranch?"

"Oh." Wacy thought for a second. "Yeah. We could take one of the old Indian trails. They wind right past some rock paintings, up to the white rock."

"Could we go there on our trail ride?" Stephanie asked.

"I don't see why not," Wacy said. "We'll have to check with Buck . . . but if we start out early enough in the morning, we can get there by noon, and have a few hours to rest before heading back."

"Did you say rock paintings?" Mr. Kessler asked. He and Nana had been busy loading their cameras. "Indian pictographs?"

"That's right. Indian braves with bows and arrows, herds of buffalo and antelopes, dancers wearing feathers," Wacy said. "They're painted in red under a big overhang on the cliff."

"I'd love to see them," Mr. Kessler exclaimed. "Sign me up for that trail ride! I've always been interested in American Indian art," he explained to Nana. "Why don't you come, too?"

"If you find me a calm horse," Nana said with a laugh. "I haven't been on one in twenty-five or thirty years."

"How about Greedy?" I suggested eagerly. I was really hoping to graduate to something a little livelier before the trip was over.

"Yes, Nana — if Greedy were any calmer, you wouldn't know he was even alive!" Stephanie said with a giggle.

"All right," Nana nodded. "We'll make a party of it. The Murphys would probably come, too. . . ."

"And the Foleys?" Stephanie suggested innocently.

Kate gave Stephanie a suspicious look.

"I don't think they ride," Nana said. "But I'll certainly mention the trail to them — particularly Tower Rock, with all its fossils. I'm sure Keith wouldn't want to miss that."

"I'm sure he wouldn't." Stephanie smiled smugly at Kate.

Patti looked at me and raised her eyebrows.

"It sounds great," I said weakly. There was no stopping Stephanie — we'd just have to make the best of it.

Chapter
7

Once we'd gotten settled, Nana and Mr. Kessler said they were going to explore the other end of the island. Kate, Stephanie, Patti, and I drank lemonade in the shade of a cottonwood tree and listened to Wacy talk about riding.

"Now when you're breaking a horse, you might think the chanciest part would be falling off," he told us. "You know — snapping your neck or something. But I think instinct helps you land clear — most of the time, anyway. No, to me, the chanciest part of riding is whether or not the horse is going to step on you once you're on the ground. Horses weigh around twelve hundred pounds, so they can do a lot of damage."

"But that could happen any time," Patti pointed out. "The horse wouldn't necessarily have to be bucking, would it?"

"Nope. Your saddle could loosen and you could slip off sideways, or the horse could stop short, like Smokey did with me this morning. Once I even had a horse step on my foot when I was bridling him," Wacy said. "I couldn't get that horse to move! Broke three toes on my right foot before Buck managed to shove him off me."

"Twelve hundred pounds!" Stephanie exclaimed — she's always worrying about her weight. "Who needs to diet? How about a sandwich?"

We ate the turkey sandwiches Mrs. Franklin had packed for us and listened to the sounds of the river and the birds singing, until Nana and Mr. Kessler got back.

Wacy squinted up at the sun, which was starting to sink toward the rim of the canyon. "I guess we'd better get going," he announced.

We packed up the picnic stuff, pulled on our life jackets, and climbed back into the raft. Wacy got into position near the motor. He pushed the starter, but nothing happened. He pushed it again. It made a low wheezing sound like someone faking a cough.

"Fuel line's probably plugged up," he said. "Nothing to worry about."

Wacy unhooked the line, blew into it, and stuck it back together. Then he tried the starter again. Still nothing.

He smiled at us encouragingly. "You folks want to climb out while I tinker with this for a second? Then we'll be on our way."

Nana, Stephanie, Kate, Patti, and I sat on an old log near the river's edge, while Mr. Kessler helped Wacy. You could hear them mumbling things like "points," and "carburetor," but each time Wacy tried the starter, nothing happened. The floor of the canyon was getting dark, and all of us were beginning to get worried.

"I think there's a flashlight stowed in the raft," Wacy said. He found it under a seat and clicked it on. Then he shook his head. "The batteries are too weak to help much," he said, shining it on the motor.

"What do we do now?" Mr. Kessler asked.

"Wait. When we don't show up at the lodge, Buck will come for us in the other raft," Wacy said.

Kate, Stephanie, Patti, and I looked at each other. It could be several hours before they started to wonder about us at the ranch, and hours more before they could reach us, down the river in the dark.

I remembered the coyotes we'd heard the night before. I didn't know about the others, but I really wasn't looking forward to a sleepover in the middle of the wilderness! I shivered and pulled my sweater around me.

As if he'd read my mind, Wacy said, "You couldn't pick a safer place to be stranded than this island. There aren't any big animals living on it and the river's much too swift for anything to swim across at this point."

Nana and Mr. Kessler agreed about the wildlife. "All we saw on our walk were hundreds of birds and one turtle," Nana said.

"Now I'm going to build a nice, big fire," Wacy said. "We can eat the rest of the sandwiches, and Buck'll be here in no time," he promised. He started gathering dead branches and stacking them up. "I'm just sorry we don't have any hot dogs or marshmallows."

The shadows in the canyon grew longer and blacker. But Wacy soon had a blazing fire going. The seven of us gathered in a circle and shared the five sandwiches that were left and the rest of Mrs. Franklin's lemonade. Then Mr. Kessler suggested we sing a few songs. It was kind of a corny idea, but it was a good one, too, because it took our minds off our predicament.

We sang "She'll be Comin' 'Round the Mountain," "On Top of Old Smokey," and a couple of other songs. We were just finishing "My Darling Clementine" when Stephanie noticed something funny.

"Look — just outside the circle of firelight," she said, pointing over Wacy's cowboy hat. "See those funny little shiny things?"

There were about twenty or thirty of them, in pairs. They looked like tiny Christmas-tree lights, if Christmas-tree lights had been strung along the ground.

"How lovely," Nana cried. "What are they, Wacy? Dew drops?"

Wacy squinted briefly into the darkness. "It's just spiders, attracted by the fire," he said. "What you're seeing are their eyes shining in the light."

"Sp-spider eyes!" Stephanie shrieked, practically jumping into my lap.

I wasn't too crazy about the idea, either, especially since the spiders seemed to be zipping back and forth as fast as if they were on roller skates!

"They wouldn't harm a fly," Wacy said quickly. "Well . . . maybe a fly . . . but not a person. They're absolutely nonpoisonous."

"What kind are they?" Patti asked in her most scientific tone. She belongs to the Quarks, a science club whose members are some of the smartest kids at Riverhurst elementary.

"Uh . . . desert tarantulas," Wacy mumbled. "They're pretty common around here, at night."

"TARANTULAS!" Stephanie, Patti, and I stampeded for the raft, leaving Kate, Nana, Mr. Kessler, and Wacy sitting by the fire.

"But they're not poisonous!" Kate called after us. "Wacy just said so!"

"Who needs poison? I'd die of fright if one got within ten feet of me!" Stephanie screeched back. "I don't know about you guys," she said to Patti and me, "but I'm not stepping out of this raft into a swarm of tarantulas, nonpoisonous or not!"

"That goes double for me," I said.

Patti nodded and swallowed hard.

So the three of us sat hunched up in the raft, getting chillier and chillier. Meanwhile, Kate and the others sat right beside the warm fire, ignoring the little gleams of light zipping all around them.

61

"I'm going to strangle Kate for being so logical," Stephanie said, shivering.

I knew exactly what she meant. Sometimes Kate's mind over matter attitude can be positively infuriating.

But Patti was more disgusted with herself. "What kind of scientist will I make," she wailed, "if I can't even stand to be around some absolutely non-poisonous spiders!"

The moon rose, and the coyotes started their weird howling.

Suddenly Patti whispered, "Do you guys hear that?"

The coyote chorus died down for a second, and the hum of an engine came bouncing off the canyon walls.

"Yay! We're saved!" Stephanie cheered.

Sure enough, a voice boomed out across the water, "Wacy? Are you stuck on the island?"

" 'Fraid so, Buck," Wacy hollered back.

A couple of minutes later, the other raft chugged into view, a spotlight beaming from the front of it and a lantern dangling from the back. Buck was steering. I could just make out Mr. Foley's gray crewcut, and . . . "Who's the third person?" I asked.

"I think it's . . . Keith!" Stephanie cried. "Isn't it the most romantic thing you've ever seen?" she added in a whisper to Patti and me. "I couldn't have planned it better myself. He's coming out here to rescue Kate!"

"I don't care who's rescuing whom," I said, "as long as we get back to our cabin tonight."

As soon as their raft bumped up on the shore of the island, Buck and Mr. Foley hopped out. Keith lurked behind in the shadows, and he stayed there while Buck and Mr. Foley tied our raft to theirs.

Nana and Mr. Kessler climbed into the lead raft with the Foleys for the trip back. Kate, Stephanie, Patti, and I stayed in our raft with Wacy, although Stephanie couldn't resist saying, "Kate, are you sure you don't want to ride in front?"

"Why should I?" Kate said, glaring slit-eyed at Stephanie.

But Stephanie couldn't resist trying once more as we headed upriver. "Don't you think Keith was brave to come for us, in the dark and everything?" she asked.

"Buck came for us," Kate pointed out sensibly.

"Kate's the one who's brave," Patti said, still upset at herself for the spider scare.

"Oh, I don't know about that," Kate mumbled.

"One thing's for sure," I said. "That island definitely has a name now."

"What?" Stephanie asked.

"Tarantula Island!"

Chapter
8

Stephanie had to give up on the idea of getting Kate and Keith together that night. As soon as we reached the ranch, we fell into bed, and within minutes we were all fast asleep.

The next morning after a quick breakfast at the lodge, it was time for another riding lesson. We led our horses out of their stalls, and curried, saddled, and bridled them. (After Wacy's story, I was careful to keep an eye out for a three-hundred-pound hoof!) Then, just after we'd mounted, and were getting to the good part, Kate came down with another headache.

First she turned pale, then she flushed. "I'm

really sorry," she told Buck, "but my head's starting to hurt again." And before we'd even ridden into the pen, Kate got down off Sal and walked back to the cabin.

"Maybe she's allergic to horse hair," Patti said to me as we trotted our horses around.

"*I* think it's Keith Foley, not allergies at all!" Stephanie said. "Look — there he goes. Now tell me that's a coincidence!"

Keith was hurrying past the horse pen toward the lodge. He held his hammer in one hand and a couple of rocks in the other.

"Thanks for saving us last night!" Stephanie called out.

Keith kind of ducked his head. His ears turned a bright red.

He was about to dash off when Buck called out, "Son, the girls are talking to you."

Keith stopped and nodded at us awkwardly.

"I think Kate's looking for you, Keith," Stephanie said.

"She wants to tell you about the fossils we saw yesterday," I added.

"She's probably up at the lodge," Patti barely managed to squeak out.

That sent Keith darting out of sight behind the stable.

"Kate's gonna kill us!" I groaned.

"Let's get riding, girls," Buck said firmly.

Patti, Stephanie, and I trotted around until our teeth rattled. Then Buck let us gallop around the pen! It was terrific, kind of like being in a rocking chair. I wasn't nearly as scared as I thought I'd be. When Buck decided we'd had enough, he said approvingly, "I think you've outgrown Greedy, Lauren. Tomorrow we'll try you out on Nifty." Nifty was a pretty brown horse with a streak down his face and a lot more energy than Greedy had!

I was feeling great about myself, but I was worried about Kate. "If she comes down with a headache — or Keith Foleyitis — every time she gets near a horse, she won't be able to go on the trail ride," I said to Stephanie and Patti as we headed up to the lodge. "And if she can't go, we shouldn't, either."

"Listen," Stephanie said. "Once I get her and Keith talking I promise the headaches won't be a problem!"

Stephanie went into action as soon as we sat down to lunch. "Keith Foley was looking for you —

he wanted to hear about the fossil rock,'' she murmured to Kate.

Kate was furious! "He actually said that, *right*,'' she growled under her breath. "He opened his mouth and spoke those exact words?''

"Well . . . uh . . . not exactly,'' Stephanie admitted.

"Some people have more important things on their minds than boys, Stephanie Green!'' Kate hissed. "So would you do me a favor — and poor Keith Foley, too — and KNOCK IT OFF!''

I looked over at Patti and sighed. "This is getting to sound a lot like the old days, and I don't mean the *good* old days,'' I whispered.

But Kate wasn't finished. "If you're such an expert on romance,'' she whispered crossly, "why don't you recognize it when it's right under your nose!'' Then she stood up and stalked away from the table without even waiting for dessert.

"Well, excu-u-use me!'' Stephanie muttered. She sulked for a minute. Then her curiosity won over her temper. "What did she mean, anyway, 'right under my nose'?''

I was wondering myself, but I didn't have an answer.

* * *

That afternoon, Patti, Stephanie, and I rode our horses up the canyon with the Murphys and another couple staying at the lodge, and Buck. Meanwhile, Kate avoided us by going hiking with Nana and Mr. Kessler.

After dinner that night, we all hung around the lodge for a while, looking at some of the funny old books in the tall bookcases — all of us except for Kate, that is. She said she didn't feel too well and walked back to the cabin by herself. When we came in, she was already in bed and didn't even open her eyes.

I was sound asleep, dreaming about roller-skating spiders chasing me down a big river, when a sound nudged me awake.

I opened one eye and blinked up at the bunk overhead. Stephanie's left leg was hanging out of the blankets, as usual, and I could hear her breathing softly.

I turned my head toward the other bunks . . . and saw that Kate's bed was empty! A creaking noise drew my attention to our bedroom door. It swung open, and Kate came through it. There was enough moonlight shining through the windows for me to see that she had on jeans and a sweatshirt. She was carrying the big flashlight Mrs. Franklin had left for Nana.

Just inside the door she turned and looked cautiously back at the bunk beds. Then she tiptoed across the floor to the corner where we'd piled our luggage. She reached out and stuck her hand into *my* canvas tote and put something in her pocket.

She peered over at me again, but I quickly closed my eyes. When I opened them, Kate was gone!

She must be meeting Keith, I thought. Stephanie and Patti should be in on this. But there wasn't time to wake them up.

I quickly slipped out of bed and pulled my sweats on over my pajamas. I stepped into my sneakers without even bothering to lace them and looked into the big room.

Nana was asleep on one of the pullout couches, lying on her back with her arms crossed. The front door of the cabin was open a crack. Kate must have left it that way so she wouldn't lock herself out.

I took a deep breath. Then I crept across the big room, right past Nana's feet, and slipped out the front door. Ahead, I could see a dim circle of light heading toward the stable.

The stable? A girl who was allergic to horses? I couldn't figure it out.

I dashed through the gate and after Kate, as quickly and as quietly as I could. But by the time I reached the stable, the light had disappeared. Had Kate continued up to the lodge or was she somewhere else altogether? I stopped beside the half-door at the end of the stable. I was trying to make up my mind what to do next when I heard somebody talking inside.

It was Kate's voice! I was sure of it even though it wasn't much more than a murmur. I strained to listen, but I couldn't hear Keith Foley — or anybody else — answering her. I had to get closer.

Slipping through the stable door, I tiptoed down the wide aisle that ran between the rows of stalls. As I passed Maxine, Greedy, and Timber, Kate's voice grew louder, and I saw the dim light again, shining in Sal's stall.

"Okay. So you weigh twelve hundred pounds," Kate was saying. "You could crush me in a second. But we've got to be friends. We've absolutely got to!"

Keith Foley definitely did not weigh twelve hundred pounds — Kate was talking to her horse!

Chapter 9

All of a sudden, I could feel a sneeze coming on. I tried to stop it by doing a trick my dad taught me — pressing on the roof of my mouth with the tip of my tongue. Sometimes it actually works, but not that night. I sneezed so loud that it even made Greedy flinch.

The dim light switched off. The stable was absolutely quiet, except for Greedy chowing down on some hay.

"Kate?" I whispered. "Kate — it's me — Lauren."

Kate didn't say anything. She just sighed and switched the light back on.

I walked down the aisle until I reached Sal's stall

door. I peered over the top. Kate was squeezed into one corner of the stall. Sal was standing in the middle of it, blinking sleepily. A slice of apple was hanging out of the horse's mouth.

"You got it," Kate said, although I hadn't said anything. "I'm bribing her with one of Mrs. Franklin's lunch apples."

"Aren't you afraid of getting a headache?" I asked.

"I made the headaches up," Kate said.

So Stephanie was right! But where was Keith? I glanced around the stable, half expecting to see him pop out of a corner. Then Kate added glumly, "What I'm afraid of is the *horse*."

I couldn't believe it! "You?" I said. "The girl who can sit through *Deadly Vampires from the Crypt*, not to mention coyote choruses and a tarantula swarm, with no problem at all?"

"Yeah, well . . . you know how I'm always teasing you about your runaway imagination?" Kate said. "I've finally realized what it means to have one. As soon as I get near this horse, I think of all the awful things that could happen. I think how she could throw me off, or run away with me, or fall down and crush me, or a million other horrible accidents, including — thanks to Wacy's story — getting stepped on."

"But Buck wouldn't give us any horse that was dangerous to ride," I told her.

Kate sighed. "I *know* that when I'm being logical." She held out another slice of apple to Sal. "Logic just doesn't last very long when it comes to horses. They're so *big*!"

I opened the stall door and walked toward the corner where Kate was sitting. That's when it happened. I'm not usually clumsy, but that night I was half asleep, plus I'd forgotten to tie my sneakers when I'd slipped into them back at the cabin.

I stepped on the loose laces of my right shoe with my left foot. Before I knew it, I went crashing down, my head knocking against the side of the horse. When I looked up I was lying under Sal — all twelve hundred pounds of her!

"Lauren!" Kate gasped.

I was feeling pretty breathless myself. The stall floors were concrete, with just a thin layer of sand on top, and I'd fallen like a tree. I didn't know whether I should freeze or scramble backward as fast as I could before Sal decided to kick me. Would she kick me if I lay very still, or was she more likely to kick a moving target?

"Kate. . . ," I wailed softly.

Sal snorted gently. She put her head down and gazed at me solemnly with one velvety brown eye. She nosed my sweatshirt. . . . Then she lifted her head and stretched her neck out for more apple. The rest of her body could have been carved in stone. She didn't twitch a single muscle.

"I think you can crawl out, Lauren," Kate murmured cautiously, giving Sal a slice of apple.

I got up on my hands and knees and carefully backed out from under the big horse.

"Whew!" I climbed to my feet. My heart was pounding so hard I thought my eardrums might burst.

Kate grinned at me. "Okay, Lauren — you've convinced me Sal is safe," she said. "But did you really have to throw yourself under her to prove it?"

Then she reached into her pocket. "Here. I borrowed this out of your tote, but I don't think I'll be needing it any more."

She handed me my lucky coin.

"And thanks," Kate said.

* * *

It was around four o'clock in the morning by that time — Kate was wearing her watch. Since we'd have to get up in another couple of hours anyway, we decided to stay at the stable.

"I want to get as used to Sal as I can before the real lesson," Kate said. "After all, I have two whole days to make up."

"Listen, we don't have to say anything to Stephanie and Patti about this, if you don't want to," I told Kate.

"No. You know what a mess it makes when we keep secrets from each other," Kate replied, stroking Sal's nose. "Besides," she added with a giggle, "telling the truth is the only way I'll ever get Stephanie to believe that I'm *not* interested in Keith Foley."

"You're not?" I exclaimed.

"Oh, Lauren!" Kate groaned. "Not you, too!"

Kate brushed Sal's coat and led her up and down the stable aisle for a while. At five, we walked over to the lodge and ate blueberry muffins fresh from the oven. The sun was just rising and the whole canyon looked pale pink and silver. Then we went back to the stable and watched Wacy getting a colt used to the saddle. By the time Stephanie and Patti showed up, we'd been awake for three hours.

"We wondered where you were," Stephanie said with a yawn. "What are you guys doing up so early?"

"Aren't you even going to eat breakfast?" Patti asked us.

"We had muffins at the — " I began.

"Lauren, are those your *pajamas* hanging out of the bottom of your sweats?" Stephanie interrupted, staring down at my feet. "What's going on?"

"I have a confession to make," Kate said.

"You *do* like Keith Foley!" Stephanie crowed. "I knew it!"

"No," Kate said. "It's *not* about Keith Foley." Then she told Stephanie and Patti about being afraid to ride.

"I was sure you'd think I was a wimp, after all of my mind-over-matter speeches," Kate said. "So I pretended I was having allergy headaches to get myself out of the riding lessons."

"What were you so embarrassed about at the lodge that first morning?" Stephanie asked her.

"I was the one who was reading *Beginner's Guide to Western Riding*, not Keith," Kate said. "I was trying to get my nerve up, but I didn't want to admit it. I thought you guys would think I was a total chicken.''

"It's no big deal," Stephanie said distractedly. I could tell her mind was still on Keith Foley, and so was mine. We'd solved the mystery about Kate, but what about Keith? If he didn't like Kate and hate the rest of us, what was *his* problem? "Everybody's scared of something," Stephanie went on. "Like tarantulas, or being seen with frizzy hair by the cutest boy in town, or — "

"The important thing is, you're getting over it!" Patti said. "We still have four days till the trail ride, and you'll be great by then."

"Maybe you're not the only one who's gearing up for the ride," Stephanie said thoughtfully. "Do you guys see what I see?"

She pointed to a clearing past the pen, where Wacy was giving someone a private riding lesson.

"The Mystery Man himself!" I said.

It was Keith Foley, climbing onto a short, white horse!

Chapter 10

The morning of the trail ride was bright and clear. After a big breakfast of pancakes and sausages at the lodge, everybody went down to the stable to saddle up: Kate, Stephanie, Patti, and I, Nana, Mr. Kessler, the Murphys, the Putnams . . . and Keith Foley. That made eleven horses, and Buck and Wacy's made thirteen. The pack horse made fourteen all together. Buck got on his brown-and-white Appaloosa, rode out front, and yelled "Move 'em out!" All of us fell into line behind him.

With Buck in the lead and Wacy at the end of the line with the pack horse, we headed up the canyon, following the river as far as we could. I was riding Nifty. He moved along briskly, his brown ears twitching back and forth as he trotted. Then Stephanie crowded up next to me on Maxine. "This is our last chance," she said.

"To do what?" Kate asked. She was just behind us, and she looked so relaxed sitting on Sal that you'd never guess she'd had any problems.

"To get to the bottom of the mystery behind the Mystery Man," Stephanie hissed.

We were near the front of the line of horses and riders. Keith Foley was near the end, behind Mr. Kessler and Nana, who rode Greedy.

"Has any one of us heard him say so much as a word?" Stephanie went on.

"No," I said.

Patti, who was just in front of us, turned a little and shook her head.

"Leave the guy alone, Stephanie," Kate said.

"So you *have* talked to him!" Stephanie eyed Kate triumphantly. "What's his story?"

Kate shook her head. "Stephanie, I can't — I promised."

Stephanie, Patti, and I all stared at her. But Kate wouldn't budge. Finally, Stephanie shrugged her shoulders. "It doesn't matter," she said. "Today we're going to make him talk, no matter what. When we get to Tower Rock, we'll corner him. He won't be able to run upstairs or out the door up there!"

Nana and Mr. Kessler had both brought their cameras. They snapped pictures of three deer staring out from behind a tree, a possum scuttling behind a rock, an owl sitting in a cedar, and, of course, lots of pictures of the Sleepover Friends on horseback.

As the rock cliffs loomed closer and closer, Buck led us away from the river. Before long, we were squeezing into a narrow trail that seemed to climb straight up the side of the canyon.

"Leave your reins loose, and just trust your horse, folks," Buck called out. "He'll pick the best place to step."

Soon we were higher than the treetops in the valley below. Then we rose even higher than some of the flying birds. All of Lost Valley stretched out beneath us. In the distance, the river looked like a shiny silver ribbon, and we could see the stable and horse pen, and even farther away, the lodge, with a wisp of gray smoke hanging over the chimney.

We kept climbing until we reached a kind of a shelf of rock under an enormous overhang.

"We'll stop here for a few minutes," Buck announced. "If you want to dismount, I'll show you some of the Indian paintings."

The rocks under the overhang were covered with them, dark-red stick figures of men shooting arrows at huge buffalos and antelopes running for their lives. There were pictures of deer leaping over rivers, and outlines of human hands.

"How old are they?" Patti asked Mr. Kessler, who used about three rolls of film, photographing the paintings.

"At least a thousand years old," he answered.

"Wow!" Stephanie was too impressed to notice that Keith Foley was crouched down just behind her. She missed cornering him.

We climbed on our horses again to finish the ride to Tower Rock. The sun, moving higher in the sky, was beating down on us. Birds were singing above and below us. The river sparkled in the canyon. It must have been seventy degrees at least, not the ten degrees it was back in Riverhurst. I sighed — I was really going to be sorry to leave Lost Valley.

My stomach had started to growl when Buck finally hollered, "Tower Rock is just up ahead. We'll eat lunch, and you'll have time to do some exploring."

The trail turned a corner, and Nifty stepped out onto a wide, grassy ledge high above the canyon floor. With some moaning and groaning, we all got off our horses and stretched our legs.

But Patti was already exploring the huge white rock that soared up the canyon wall. "Scallop shells," she said, pointing to a small, grooved fan sticking out of Tower Rock. "Barnacles. Trilobites! From fifteen million years ago, when this whole area was completely under the ocean!"

Keith Foley was standing only a few feet away, so he heard every word. He looked at Patti in total amazement . . . and smiled!

"Mystery's over," Kate murmured.

Keith's mouth glittered like a mirror. He was wearing a full set of braces, top and bottom.

"Is that all?! You could have told us!" Stephanie said to Kate.

"Keith and I traded secrets," Kate replied. "He caught me reading the horse book, and I caught him taking a big bite of a muffin with all his braces showing."

"Braces are totally boring." Stephanie was totally disappointed in the truth about Keith Foley.

"Not to him," Kate said. "They're brand new,

and some of the kids at his school started calling him Ragnar."

"You mean as in *Ragnar, The Metal Monster*?" I asked, remembering a science-fiction movie we'd seen a few months before.

"You got it," Kate said.

Once he'd blown his cover, I guess Keith figured that he might as well act normal. For the rest of the trail ride, you couldn't have *pried* him away from Patti. They talked about fossils all the way back down the canyon.

But that wasn't the only news of the day. And Stephanie found the second surprise anything but boring! When we stopped at the overhang again on our way down, I noticed Nana and Mr. Kessler *holding hands.*

"My own grandmother?!" Stephanie whispered, shocked.

"Mr. Kessler is a very nice man," Kate said.

"And handsome, too," I added.

"Is that what you meant about right under my nose?"

Kate nodded.

"But she never asked for my help, the way the fortune cookie said. . . ," Stephanie protested.

"Obviously, she didn't need to," Kate reminded her. "And, judging from experience, I'd say it's a good thing. . . ."

"Well, I guess I've learned a lesson," Stephanie said sadly. "Either romances happen, or they don't. You can't plan them."

When Buck drove up to our cabin in the wagon the next morning, he wasn't alone. He had Mr. Kessler and Keith Foley with him.

"We wanted to give you a proper send-off," Mr. Kessler said to Nana as Buck piled our suitcases into the back.

Keith Foley just grinned at Patti, the sunshine glinting off his braces.

"My fortune cookie was right, after all," Stephanie murmured.

"Stephanie, you're *not* going to take credit for Nana and Mr. Kessler!" Kate exclaimed, outraged.

"No — for Patti and Keith Foley!" Stephanie replied.

"How do you figure that?" I asked her.

"Didn't I always say that the way to Keith Foley's heart was *fossils*?" Stephanie answered grandly.

We all rode to the airstrip together. The little

plane was waiting for us. The propellers started to turn before we were even out of the wagon.

Stephanie nudged me with her elbow as Mr. Kessler gave Nana a kiss on the cheek. I heard Patti yelling to Keith over the noise of the engine, "Twenty-six Mill Road," which is her address in Riverhurst.

Mr. Kessler gave all four of us a big hug. Buck shook our hands and said, "I hope you all come back real soon!" Then Keith Foley gave us all a final, glittering smile.

"Bye, girls!" he said. "Nice meeting you."

"He has a nice voice!" I whispered to Patti. She nodded without meeting my eyes.

We climbed onto the plane and strapped on our seat belts. The propellers began to spin faster and faster, and we started rolling down the runway.

I gripped the arms of my seat and squeezed my eyes shut.

Kate was sitting next to me. "Lauren," she said, "Remember, mind over ma —" But then she stopped herself. "Old habits die hard," she added with a giggle.

"I know one old habit that will last forever,"

Stephanie said from across the aisle. "The Sleepover Friends!"

We all smiled though I still kept a tight grip on the arms of my seat — just in case!

Sleepover Friends forever!

SLEEPOVER FRIENDS

#17 Patti Gets Even

"Cut it out, Wayne Miller!" I yelled, without even bothering to turn around. Wayne Miller is this awful guy in Mrs. Milton's class, 5a.

"They're reading the Winter Carnival poster, Wayne," his creepy little friend, Ronny Wallace, reported with a snicker.

"Let them look," Wayne said. "We're going to win all the prizes. Girls never win anything anyway!"

"Oh, yeah, Wayne?" Patti stopped and glared at him. "I am so totally convinced you're wrong that I'll . . . I'll personally do your next science project for you if we don't win more contests than *you* do at the Winter Carnival!"

"You got a deal!" Wayne stuck out his big, ugly hand. "Shake!"

"Shake!" Patti grabbed it and shook, hard.

Kate groaned, "Patti, have you gone crazy?"

WIN FIVE NIGHTSHIRTS FOR YOUR NEXT SLEEPOVER!

SLEEPOVER FRIENDS

Enter the SLEEPOVER FRIENDS Super Summer Giveaway

200 Winners!

"What's your favorite thing to do at a sleepover party?"

Make your next sleepover the best ever with FIVE fabulous, oversized Sleepover Friends nightshirts for you and four friends. It's easy to win! Just tell us what's *your* favorite thing to do at a sleepover party—like telling spooky ghost stories, or doing super makeovers! Then all you have to do to enter the Sleepover Friends Super Summer Giveaway is complete the coupon below and return by November 30, 1989.

Rules: Entries must be postmarked by November 30, 1989. Winners will be picked at random from all eligible entries received. No purchase necessary. Valid only in the U.S.A. Employees of Scholastic Inc., affiliates, subsidiaries, and their families are not eligible. Void where prohibited. Winners will be notified by mail.

Fill in the coupon below or write the information on a 3"x 5" piece of paper and mail to: SLEEPOVER FRIENDS SUPER SUMMER GIVEAWAY, Scholastic Inc., P.O. Box 665, Cooper Station, New York, NY 10276.

Sleepover Friends Super Summer Giveaway

What's your favorite thing to do at a sleepover party?

Check one:
- ☐ Eating
- ☐ Makeovers
- ☐ Cooking
- ☐ Truth or Dare
- ☐ Telling Ghost Stories
- ☐ Other _____

Name _____ Age _____

Street _____

City, State, Zip _____

Where did you buy this *Sleepover Friends* book?
- ☐ Bookstore
- ☐ Book Fair
- ☐ Drug Store
- ☐ Book Club
- ☐ Supermarket
- ☐ Discount Store
- ☐ Other _____

SLE289

Pack your bags for fun and adventure with

SLEEPOVER FRIENDS™
by Susan Saunders

Join Kate, Lauren, Stephanie and Patti at their great sleepover parties every weekend. Truth or Dare, scary movies, late-night boy talk–it's all part of **Sleepover Friends!**